First published in 2013 by Child's Play (International) Ltd
Ashworth Road, Bridgemead, Swindon SN5 7YD UK

Published in USA by Child's Play Inc
250 Minot Avenue, Auburn, Maine 04210

Distributed in Australia by Child's Play Australia Pty Ltd
Unit 10/20 Narabang Way, Belrose, NSW 2085

Printed and bound in Guangzhou, China

ISBN 978-1-84643-603-1
Z190214CPL04146031

3 5 7 9 10 8 6 4

A catalogue record of this book is available from the British Library

www.childs-play.com

MOMO and SNAP

are NOT friends!

AIRLIE ANDERSON

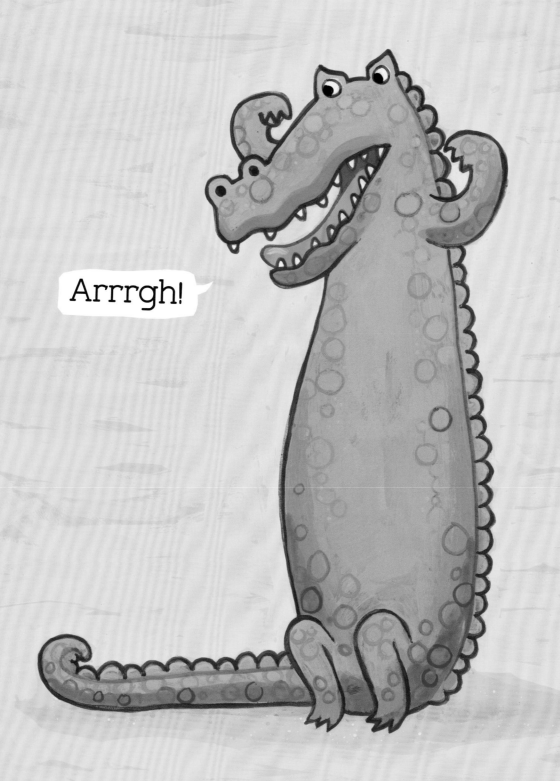

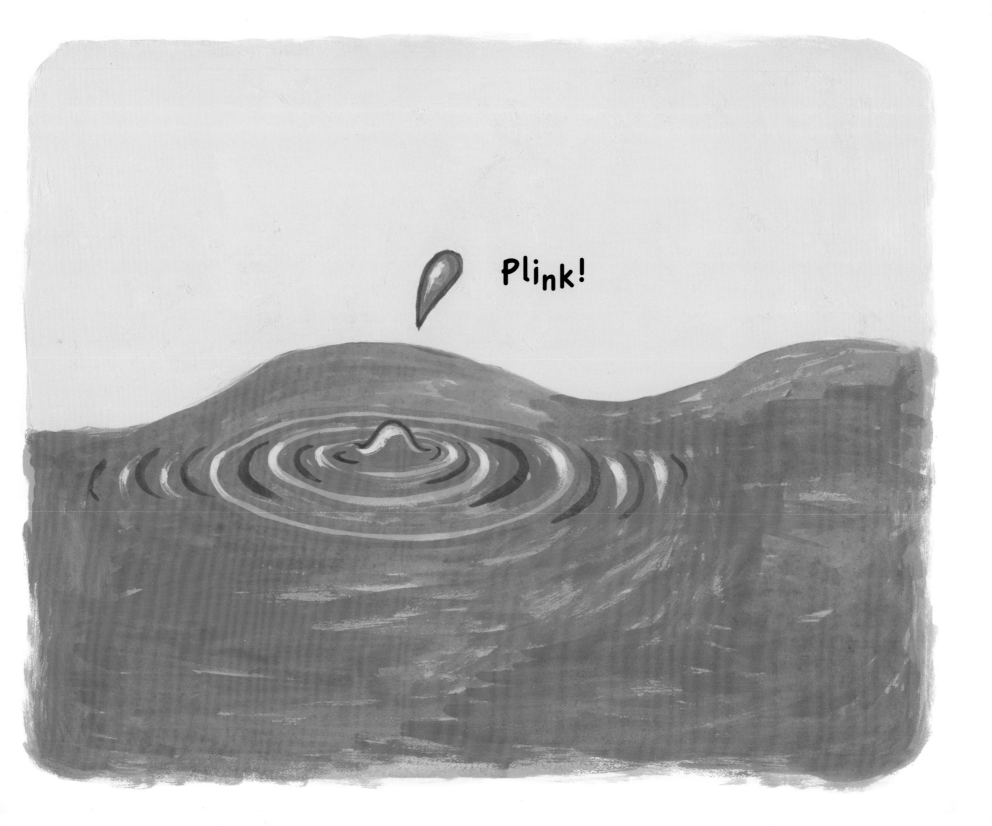

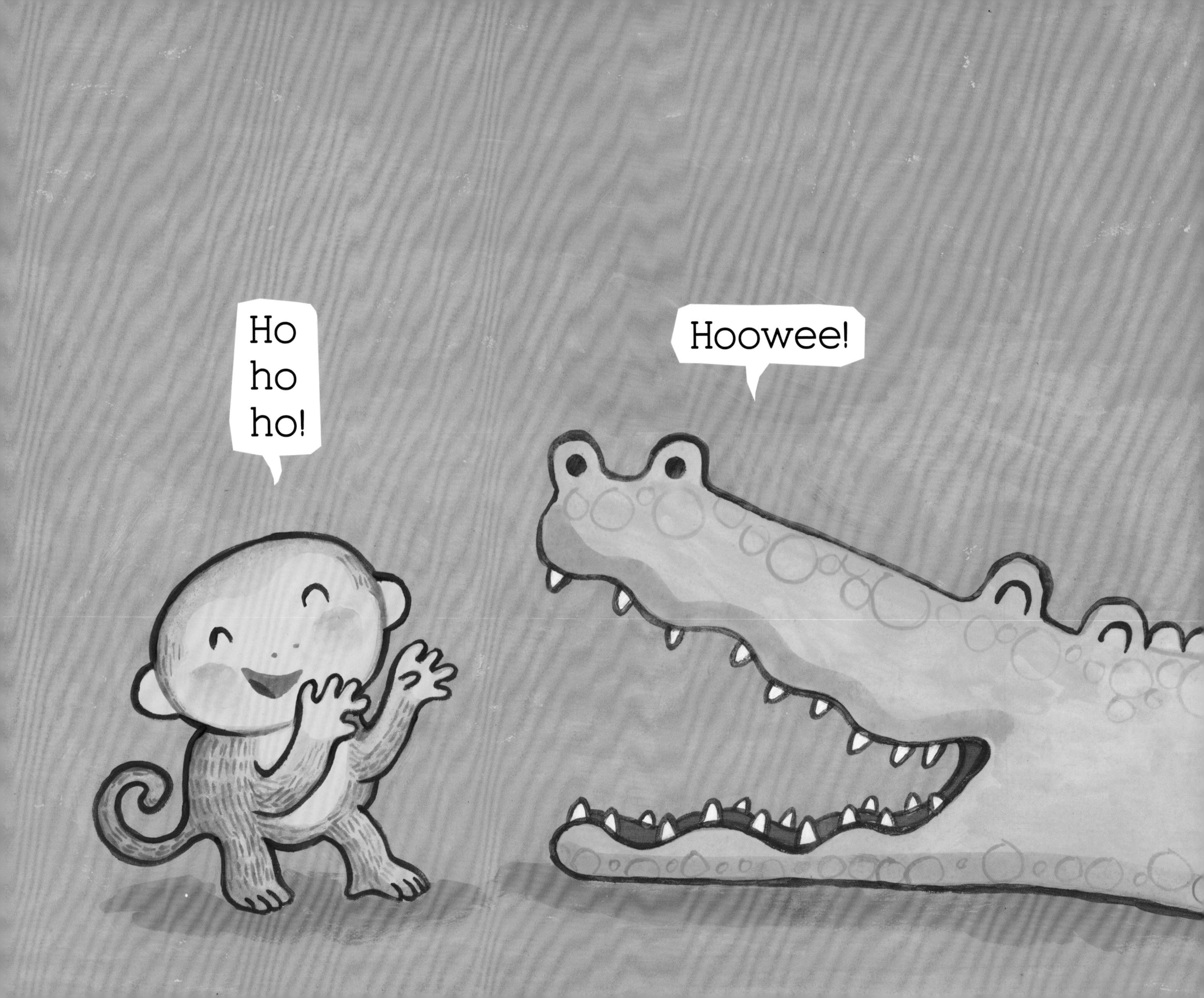
Ho
ho
ho!
Hoowee!